GURU NANAK

THE FIRST SIKH GURU

An imprint of Om Books International

First Reprint 2012

Published by

An imprint of Om Books International

Corporate & Editorial Office
A 12, Sector 64, Noida 201 301
Uttar Pradesh, India
Phone: +91 120 477 4100
Email: editorial@ombooks.com
Website: www.ombooksinternational.com

Sales Office
4379/4B, Prakash House, Ansari Road
Darya Ganj, New Delhi 110 002, India
Phone: +91 11 2326 3363, 2326 5303
Fax: +91 11 2327 8091
Email: sales@ombooks.com
Website: www.ombooks.com

ISBN : 978-81-87108-43-6

Printed in India

10 9 8 7 6 5 4 3 2

Contents

The Childhood Years

Guru Nanak Saheb was born in the year 1469 in Talwandi, which is today a part of West Pakistan. His mother was Trupta and his father was Kalu Mehta. When the naming ceremony had to be done, Kalu Mehta called for a priest. The priest studied the child's horoscope with a lot of interest. "Your son will be a

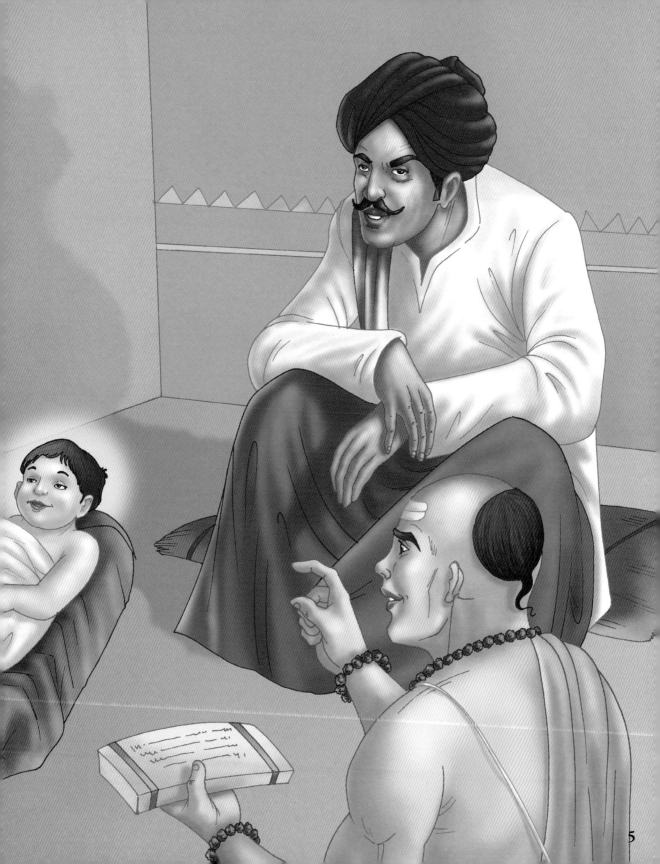

great saint one day," he said. "He will be known all over the world for his nobility and teachings," he added. Kalu Mehta and his wife were overjoyed to hear this. The child was named Nanak.

Nanak started showing signs of brilliance from an early age. He was intelligent, curious and always eager to learn. His teachers had to work very hard to answer his questions.

One day, Nanak's teacher, Pandit Gopaldas, asked him to chant the sacred syllable 'Om'. "Sir, I will chant it, but before I do so, I want you to explain its meaning to me," said young Nanak. Panditji was surprised to hear this from a young boy. "It is the

name of the Lord. He can be thought of with just one syllable, Om," replied Panditji.

"In that case, I have a new name for the Lord! I will call him Sat Kartar from today," said Nanak. Panditji was delighted to see this wisdom in such a young child and blessed him that he would become a great teacher one day.

From a young age, Nanak respected holy men (Fakirs). He would visit any gathering where Fakirs were present and listen to their teachings and hymns. Nanak's father observed that his son did not show much interest in

activities for his age. So he decided to give some responsibility to Nanak. "You will take our cattle for grazing to the forest," he told his son. Nanak was a dutiful son and agreed to do so.

The next day, Nanak took the cattle and reached the nearby forest. While they grazed on the pasture, Nanak decided to sit under a tree and meditate upon the Lord. The breeze was pleasant and Nanak soon fell asleep where he was meditating.

Unknown to him, something strange happened that day! A cobra, slid towards him and raised its hood over his head to give him shelter from the direct sunlight, which fell over his face. Nanak was fast asleep and did not realise that there was a cobra over his head!

At that time, Rai Balur, the ruler of the city where Nanak lived was passing by. "I must save that boy from being bitten," he thought and was about to move towards Nanak, when he saw the cobra sliding away

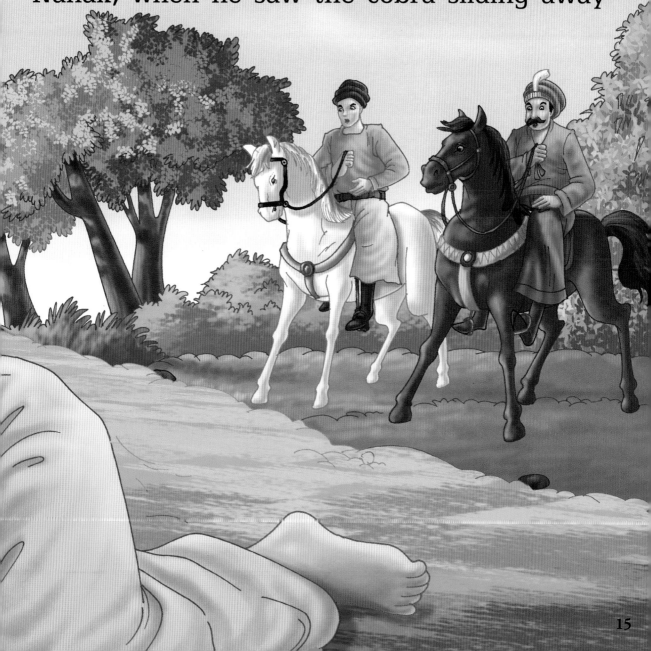

slowly. "This boy is no ordinary one," the king thought and left the place.

Nanak continued to take the cattle for grazing. And he would allow them to wander wherever they desired. One day, as the cattle went grazing into someone's fields, the owner got very angry with Nanak. "If you bring your cattle for grazing, should you not see where they are eating? They have destroyed my fields!" shouted the owner.

But Nanak was not shocked with all this. He just smiled at the incident. This angered the owner even more. So, he decided to take the matter to the king.

"Your majesty! Nanak's cattle have destroyed my field. My loss has to be made good," said the owner, seeking justice from the king. Rai Balur recognised Nanak to be the boy who had been given shade by the cobra. He looked at Nanak for an answer.

"We will measure the crops at the end of the year. If they are in anyway lesser than what they measured previous year, I will make good the loss," promised Nanak and left the court.

That year the harvest was measured and found to have doubled over the previous year! The owner rushed to Nanak's house and fell at his feet begging for forgiveness.

Family Ties

The news of the harvest doubling, spread far and wide and everyone starting talking about Nanak the Saint. Soon people started calling him Guru Nanak Saheb. Guru Nanak's father was not happy with this. He felt that his son had to get married and lead a normal life.

Sainthood was not for him! So, he decided to give him some money and asked him to start a business.

Nanak and his friend set out to start a trade. On the way they met a few hungry Fakirs. Nanak's heart ached to see them hungry. So he went to the nearby market and bought food for them.

When he returned home, Guru Nanak had to face his father. "Which trade did you decide upon?" asked his father. "Father, on my way to begin a trade, I saw some poor and needy holy men. So I bought them food with the

money you had given me," Nanak replied. "How could you do this? You have wasted my hard-earned money!" said his father angrily. "Your hard-earned money has been used to help the needy, Father," replied Nanak.

But Guru Nanak's father was very angry and started beating him. Nanki, Nanak's sister and her husband, Jai Ram, had come to pay Nanki's household a visit. They were shocked to see the sight of Nanak being beaten up.

"Father, you cannot treat my brother like a child anymore," said Nanki angrily to her father. "I will not do so, if he realises his responsibilities," replied Kalu Mehta.

News of Nanak's getting beaten up reached the ears of Rai Balur. He summoned Nanki and Jai Ram to his palace. "Nanak needs a job to settle down as a family man. Take him to Sultanpur and get him a job," said Rai Balur. "I also have a suggestion to make. Let us get Nanak married," added Nanki.

So Nanak was married to Sulakhni and left for Sultanpur, where he worked as a storekeeper in the state granary.

Daulat Khan Lodi, the ruler of Sultanpur, was very fond of Nanak.

Soon Nanak and Sulakhni were blessed with two sons. But all was not well at the granary. "Have you observed that over the years, Daulat Khan has always been partial to Nanak?" said one jealous worker to the other. "Yes, I have. It is our destiny that we are not favoured," replied the other. "Then let us change our destiny. We can always turn Daulat Khan against Nanak," said the first worker and made a plan.

They went to Daulat Khan's court and informed him that Nanak was giving away the grain freely. "One day, there will be nothing left in the granary," said the workers. Daulat Khan was shocked with this accusation. So he asked the granary and its accounts to

be thoroughly checked. But to everyone's surprise, the grain was intact and so was the money.

"Your majesty, every thing is in order. All the accusations against Nanak are false," said the state's accountant. Daulat Khan let the workers free after they pleaded for mercy on the condition that they would never repeat their evil act.

Nanak was disturbed by the incident. He went to the river for his morning bath one day, and did not return. Sulakhni and the children wept bitterly thinking that Nanak had died and left them homeless.

However, Nanak returned after three days and announced that he was not going to continue with his family life. "I have received an order from the supreme Lord to teach the path of love to people, all over the world. The purpose of my life is to spread the importance of righteousness and devotion to the Lord," said Nanak.

Though his family was not happy to see him leave, they knew that he had to do what the Lord asked him to.

And thus, Guru Nanak set out to spread the Lord's word among the people...

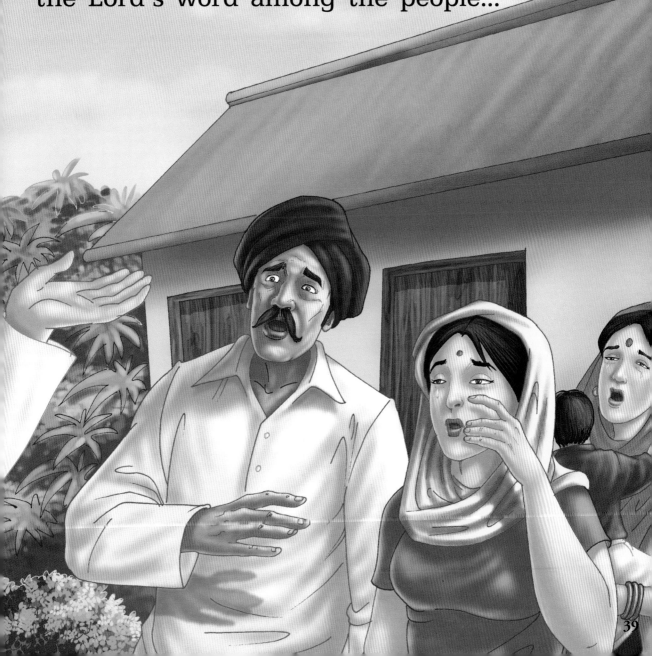

The Story of the Needle

Dunichand was a rich merchant in Lahore. His richness had made him a proud man. He had heard about Guru

Nanak and was very keen to invite him for a meal to his place. "Guruji, I am your ardent devotee, and would like to invite you for lunch," said Dunichand.

Guru Nanak accepted the invitation and reached Dunichand's house.

All through the lunch, Dunichand spoke about his riches and wealth. "The silver vessels

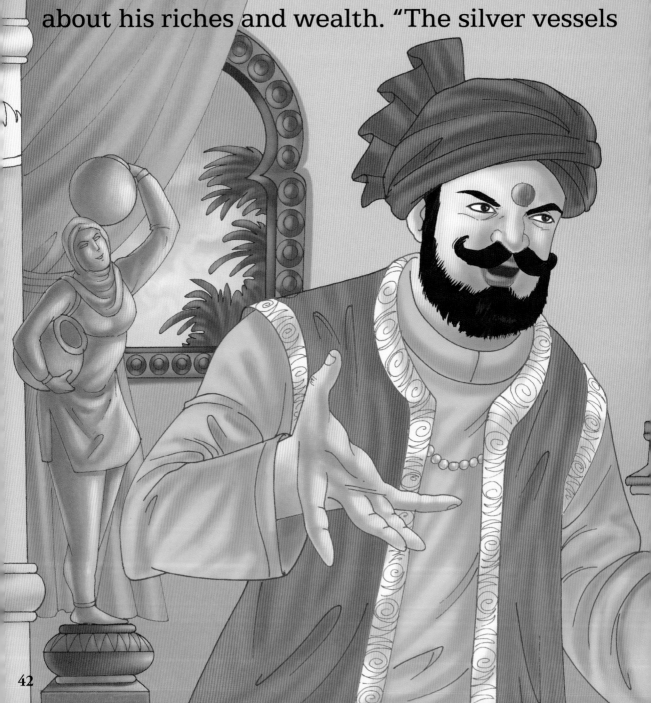

in my house are priceless," said Dunichand.
"I have the best of horses to ride around,"
added Dunichand a short while later.

Guru Nanak had his lunch quietly. At the end of the lunch, he gave Dunichand a needle. "What is this?" asked Dunichand. "It is a small needle," replied Guru Nanak. "I want you to do me a favour. When you visit me in heaven, please remember to bring this needle along," said Guru Nanak.

"How would I carry a needle after my death?" asked a surprised Dunichand. "If that is so, then what is the use of having so much wealth?" replied Guru Nanak. "We will all

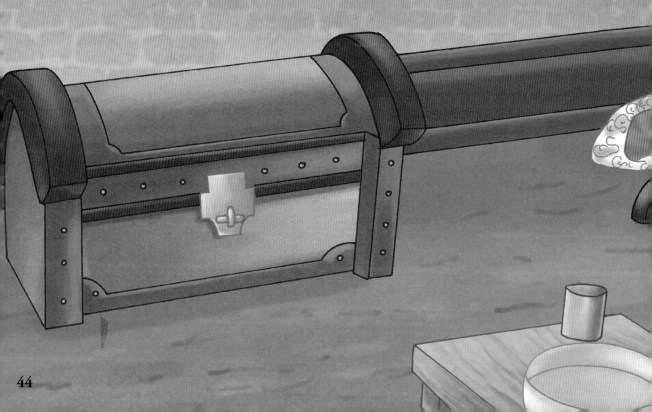

leave this world with nothing. While we are here, we must look after the poor and the needy and spread goodness all around," he advised.

Dunichand was ashamed of himself. He apologised to Guruji and promised, "From this day on, I am a changed man. I will build rest houses for the poor and distribute food and clothes to the needy."

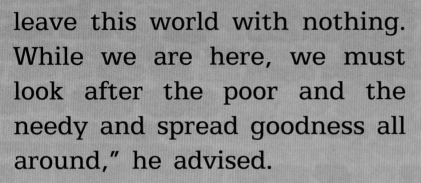

Blood or Milk?

During his travel from one place to another, Guru Nanak and his disciples reached Amanabad. There he met a carpenter by the name of Lalo Bhai.

Lalo had heard about the great teacher. He humbly invited him for a meal, "Sire, I live in a very small hut. But my family and I would be delighted if you could give us the opportunity of serving you a meal."

"It is not your hut that matters to me," said Guruji. "It is the warmth of your heart

that appeals to me. I will be delighted to have a meal at your place," he added. Lalo Bhai and his wife served Guru Nanak with great devotion.

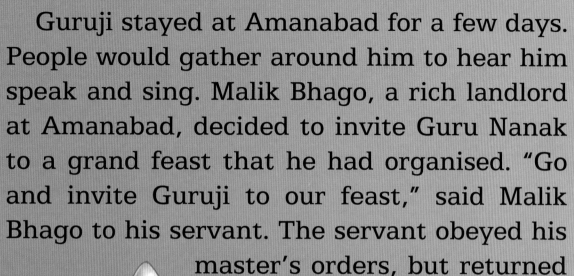

Guruji stayed at Amanabad for a few days. People would gather around him to hear him speak and sing. Malik Bhago, a rich landlord at Amanabad, decided to invite Guru Nanak to a grand feast that he had organised. "Go and invite Guruji to our feast," said Malik Bhago to his servant. The servant obeyed his master's orders, but returned a disappointed man. "Guruji has refused the invitation," said the servant. "How

could he accept a carpenter's invitation and refuse mine?" asked Bhago and stormed to meet Guru Nanak with a box of sweets.

He saw Guru Nanak eating dry rotis (Indian bread) made by Lalo Bhai. "Guruji, I have brought the best of sweets for you. Why did you refuse my invitation? You could have eaten much better food than this," said Malik Bhago arrogantly.

Guruji took one of the rotis he was eating and squeezed it. Milk started dripping from it. "Give me one of your sweets," said Guru Nanak. He squeezed the sweet and to everyone's surprise, blood started dripping from it.

"You make your workers work very hard and give them and their families nothing to eat. You make your

money from the sweat and blood of others. That is the reason for your sweet dripping blood and Lalo's dripping milk. He makes his money from working hard and shares the little he has with others," said Guru Nanak calmly.

Malik Bhago and everyone who was present were stunned at seeing this. Malik Bhago went down on his knees and wept. "Guruji, I have learnt my lesson. I will serve the poor and needy from today," he said as a changed man.

Guru Nanak Chooses His Successor

Bhai Laihna was a simple and contented man leading a happy family life. But, his heart was not at peace. He always felt the need for a teacher who could show him the right path to reach the Lord.

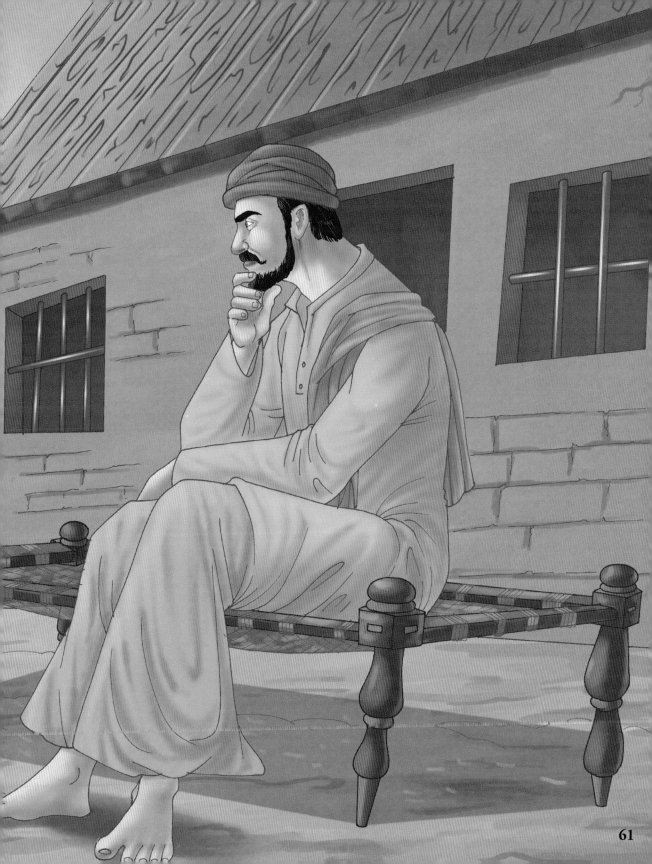

One day, he was having a bath in a river nearby, when he heard a soulful song. He looked around and saw a middle-aged man, sitting under a tree, singing. "Are you the person who wrote this song?" asked Laihna. "No, I am not the writer," replied the man. "I am singing a holy hymn written by Guru Nanak Sahebji," he added.

Laihna felt a tug from within. He felt that his pursuit for a teacher had come to an end.

He had to find Guru Nanak. "Can you tell me where he lives?" he asked the man. After taking the directions, he bid farewell to his family life and went in search of Guru Nanak. On his way, he met an old man with a white

beard. "Could you tell me where I can find Guru Nanak?" Laihna asked the old man. "Please wait for a few minutes, and then I will take you to him," answered the old man.

Laihna waited patiently, and as he had promised, the old man made Laihna sit on a horse and took him to an ashram. There he asked the man to get down and step inside to see the Guru he had been longing for. Laihna went inside and was indeed surprised to see the same old man with the white beard. "Where is Guru Nanakji?" asked Laihna. "I am

Guru Nanak, and I brought you on the horse as you are my guest, and a guest is like the Lord himself," said Guru Nanak.

Laihna's eyes were filled with tears on hearing this. He fell at Guruji's feet and said, "Now since I have found you, I want to serve you for the rest of my life."

Bhai Laihna, as he came to be known, was very devoted to Guru Nanak. When the time for finding a successor came, Guru Nanak was sure Laihna was the chosen one. But his wife had other thoughts. "Don't you think your own sons deserve a chance?" she asked Guru Nanak.

"Your feelings as a mother are right, but I am looking for a successor who can spread the love of God all over the world," replied Guru Nanak. "The Lord will help me in making the right choice," he added.

After a few days, Guru Nanak was passing by a dirty pond with his sons and disciples. He took a vessel and threw it into the pond. Then he turned to his sons. "Please bring back the vessel from the pond," said Guru Nanak. "Father, that pond has very dirty water. We have many good vessels in our house. We surely don't need to dirty ourselves trying to get this vessel," said Guru Nanak's son. Guru Nanak simply smiled. He turned to Bhai Laihna and asked him to do the same task. Without a thought, Laihna jumped into the water. After minutes, he emerged from the water with the vessel in his hand.

"What Laihna jumped into was not a mere pond," said Guru Nanak to his wife. "It was like the pond of people's sins. Your son found the pond too dirty. But Bhai Laihna did

not. What the world needs is someone like Laihna, who can save them from their sins without even thinking for a second," added Guru Nanak.

But Guru Nanak did not stop there. He went on to put his son and Laihna through another test. He asked his sons to wash his clothes on a cold, freezing morning. While his son refused, Bhai Laihna woke up immediately and promptly went to the stream to wash the clothes.

After such similar tests, Guru Nanak proved that Bhai Laihna was his chosen successor.

Guru Nanak was highly regarded by both the Hindus and Muslims. While the Hindu followers called him Guruji, his devout Muslim followers regarded him as Pir. When Guruji departed from this world, the Hindus fought

with the Muslims to perform the last rites. But, they were surprised when they removed the cloth covering his body. There was just a bed of flowers. So, the Hindus and Muslims divided the flowers between each other and returned to their homes.

Bhai Laihna succeeded Guru Nanak and came to be known as Guru Angad Dev.

TITLES IN THIS SERIES

 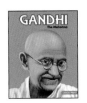